KLASSROOM KONVOS

Teacher Tales

Corinthia A. Myrick

i

Klassroom Konvos

This book is affectionately dedicated to my mother, Felicia, whose vision, love, and sacrifice in all of my educational endeavors is never less than my own.

Session 1

[*WX-309 jingle plays.*]

DJ DRIZZLE. What's up and welcome to WX-309. It's going to be a classic year! We're on a brand-new satellite radio station, and I'm here to keep you up to date with all the news in the south. We have an interesting new component in which we are highlighting what's happening at Hillsdale Middle School with Ms. Myrick, but before we get into all the new features of the show, let's check out this popping new song "2 On" by artist Tinashe.

[*DJ Drizzle plays "2 On."*]

      Great new song from Tinashe, it's going to be a classic. Now, we've got a lot of interesting things to talk about today. It's back-to-school time and this year we'll be following our favorite teacher, Ms. Myrick. She'll be teaching at thee Hillsdale Middle School. Hillsdale Middle School sits in the heart of rural South Florida. You'll find the best sugarcane in the country. You've guessed it, "her soil is her fortune". We're so happy to get a weekly account of her classroom experiences. There's a rumor going around that the older teachers at Hillsdale don't think Ms. Myrick is tough enough to handle the kids in the south, that's right, I've brought Ms. Myrick in for a chat. Tell me about your first week.

MS. MYRICK. Oh man, it's been quite an adjustment. Of course. I came down from Atlanta in March to teach seventh and eighth grade. I'm excited to start the new school year. Although August came too fast, I am prepared. Middle school is exhausting, and it ain't for everybody.

DJ DRIZZLE. You have that country accent going on [*laughs*]. Well, the audience is ready to hear about your first week of school. How was it?

MS. MYRICK. Okay, the first day of school, August 18, was pretty harmless. The kids are trying to figure me out. I had one that tried me, and I simply said, "See, you came to school to play, and I'm NOT playing with you. You may need a schedule change, son." After that little incident, we analyzed *Invictus*, and they requested I bring more poems like that. We also learned how to walk down the hallway a million times quietly. Tests will be held on Wednesdays and Fridays to get them in the habit of studying. They are upset now, but they will be happy later. One of the hardest things about teaching middle school is keeping a straight face and not laughing when they are talking junk to their peers. It takes some serious self-control. Kids are so mean to each other!

DJ DRIZZLE. Well, it seems like you're laying the hammer to them. Let's play that hit "No Type" from Rae Sremmurd before we find out how you're enjoying the palm trees in sunny South Florida.

[*DJ Drizzle plays "No Type."*]

DJ DRIZZLE. [*Fades out "No Type."*] How are you adjusting to the new city?

MS. MYRICK. Well, I finally went driving just to drive, crazy right, to learn West Palm Beach. This is a very nice place, no complaints as far as the actual city is concerned. Well, there are three: there isn't a Zaxbys, the driving down here is God awful, and I still don't know how I feel about tornados and hurricanes. I miss my family and friends, something terrible. If I can move them here, I'll be okay! So, who's moving here first?! Lol, just kidding.

I'll keep my three to five-year plan before I make any drastic decisions. Luckily, there is an ease to all the separation anxiety; everybody has been stopping in to visit. I will say it's extremely different from Atlanta because *everyday* someone asks me, "What country are you from? You from the islands?" Or my favorite, "You look like an African princess," Lol. I simply respond with, "I was born in Atlanta, Georgia." The people asking seem so irritated with my response, but I don't want to lie. I should probably do some research and trace my roots or something.

Other than that, DJ Drizzle, I wake up every morning in awe. I'm twenty-three with the career that I've always wanted. I often fear the unknown, but you can't pray and worry. My pilot has not steered me wrong, and I just can't wait for what's ahead. Until then, I'll just keep pressing forward. "The only tragedy isn't death; it's living life without purpose." I don't know who said that quote, but I live by it.

DJ DRIZZLE. So, what have you been finding to do for fun?

MS. MYRICK. Look, I normally just drive around to find good food, do homework, and binge- watch *Orange Is the New Black*. I have had conch in every way you can possibly make it. Tonight, I had stewed conch and nearly slapped somebody, Lol. Lawd have mercy! Won't He do it?! They don't sell food like that in Atlanta.

DJ DRIZZLE. You watch *Orange Is the New Black*? Man, did you finish the season?

MS. MYRICK. Of course, I did. My favorite quote on the last episode is definitely, "Stop, don't talk to me, loser, lame boy, wanna be, oh, like totally, all you want to be is me...stay fresh."

DJ DRIZZLE. [*Laughing*] Those women are most definitely off their rockers. It's an awesome show. I hope they get another season! It looks like we might be out of time. Let's thank Ms. Myrick for stopping in this week and letting us know how things are going over at the middle school. You can catch Ms. Myrick each and every week as she delivers her stories in the classroom in a unique and very special way. We'll see you next week! And with that, we have to pay these bills. As always, thanks for rocking out with ya boy, DJ Drizzle.

Session 2

[*WX-309 jingle plays.*]

DJ DRIZZLE. What's good in the Dirty, Dirty?! We're on a brand-new satellite radio station, and I'm here to keep you up to date with all the news in the south. Last week we introduced Ms. Myrick, and she's going to be highlighting what's happening at a local middle school throughout the year, but before we get to Ms. My, let's check out what's popping with "Fight Night" by the Migos.

[*DJ Drizzle plays "Fight Night."*]

DJ DRIZZLE. [*Fades out "Fight Night."*] Ms. My, how you doing over there?

MS. MYRICK. Is it fall break yet? It's only been roughly a week and a half of school, and it's time for a break!

DJ DRIZZLE. What's going on in that school, man?

Ms. Myrick. Well, I can't use any student names, so they'll always be Student A, B, or C. Sometimes, it will be the same student, most times, it won't. I'll give you stories for the week. Deal?

DJ Drizzle Deal.

Ms. Myrick. We're settling into the classroom expectations, but it's middle school. The students are still trying to figure me out. We're discussing their summer reading, "The Pact," and Student A raises her hand,

> Student A: "Ms., you pregnant?"

> Me: "No. Why would you ask that?"

> Student A: "Only pregnant women drink a lot of orange juice."

> Me: "Is that right?"

> Student A: "Yeah, so you got a boyfriend? How many kids you got? What you having?"

Me: "What's the central idea of 'The Pact,' and what are the supporting details?"

DJ DRIZZLE. Woah, they went for it, huh? That's wild!

MS. MYRICK. Man, if only they knew there's nobody checking for me and I am not even close to being pregnant! Everybody is marrying me off and placing these kids on me; I'm glad they have hope. Praying for a ram in the bush.

DJ DRIZZLE. Wait a minute, wait a minute! Let's play a song that the kids know all too well, "0 to 100" by ya boy, Drake.

[*DJ Drizzle plays "0 to 100."*]

DJ DRIZZLE. [*Fades out "0 to 100."*] So, your kids are already showing their true colors. Did anything happen that was eye-opening to you?

MS. MYRICK. September 16, 2014, will be sketched into my memory. We had a talk about cultures. The atmosphere was relaxed and calm, and the students were comfortable. I noticed one of my students did not participate in the conversation. I asked him about his culture, and he said he moved here from Asia. He isn't Asian. In fact, he is from Saudi Arabia. I asked him why he wanted to identify with the Asian culture, and he looked at me with tears in his eyes and said, "Everybody thinks I am a terrible person." He continued saying, "It is easier for me to hide." I thought to myself this is your moment! I looked at him, and I gave him an emotional, motivational speech. Needless to say, all his classmates were asking him questions, and he was delighted to tell them about his culture; I almost shed a thug tear. I've had Asian, Mexican, and Haitian students, but this was my first student from Saudi Arabia, and the first time I've had a teenage boy have a total meltdown in front of me.

DJ DRIZZLE. It sounds like you wear many hats as an educator.

MS. MYRICK. Of course, of course. But that's what keeps me moving in this field.

DJ DRIZZLE. We need a lot more teachers that have that same ambition. That's dope. I'm a little disappointed we couldn't get another story in, but there's always next week! Let's pay these bills y'all.

Session 3

[WX-309 jingle plays.]

DJ DRIZZLE. Oh, what a time to be alive! We have our favorite teacher, Ms. Myrick, back and she's going to be highlighting what's happening at the middle school, but before we get to Ms. My, let's check out what's popping with "Anaconda" by Ms. Nicki Minaj.

[DJ Drizzle plays "Anaconda."]

DJ DRIZZLE. *[Fades out "Anaconda."]* Before you get started, let me just say, I've literally been waiting on this all day. What's going on in that school Mih My?!

MS. MYRICK. Well, today was a school-wide literacy day. Every teacher in seventh grade had to give a lesson on immigrants. It was hilarious because articles talked about polygamy and anarchist, explaining polygamy was awesome. Anyway, I asked all the students, which are 40% Haitian and 40% Hispanic, to raise their hands if they are immigrants. They were scared at first, but then this boy bursts out and says, "Ms. Myrick, aren't we all immigrants?! We

weren't originally here!" HELLO,
SOMEBODY! These kids actually   listen
to me. If I could hit a two-step in class, I
would have. Now, I just have to figure out
how to process this little boy telling me he
wants to be a lesbian when he gets older.
Never a dull day!

DJ DRIZZLE. Uh-oh, Ms. Myrick, you
putting the kids on, huh? I'm not sure if
anybody wants to hear any music right now,
but let's get into this "Fancy" by Iggy.

[*DJ Drizzle plays "Fancy."*]

DJ DRIZZLE. [*Fades out "Fancy."*] Ms.
Myrick, Ms. Myrick. You're shaking tables.

MS. MYRICK. I'd just like for my students to
think critically is all. I mean it's an intensive
reading strategy, I just want them to have
real-life application skills, you know?

DJ DRIZZLE. It sounds good, but I see where
it's going.

MS. MYRICK. Well, I have to put in a lot of
work because later on in the week, my
morning started with a young man bursting
into tears because he wasn't paying attention
and was embarrassed when the class

chastised him. He cried for an hour before I got annoyed with him and asked him to step outside. He told the assistant principal on me. I had a fight break out in class because one boy pinched another boy's nipples. It ended with my darling student telling me I didn't have common sense because I sweep the floor with a broom, and I'm supposed to broom with a broom because you mop with a mop. I'm just glad the holiday is near!

DJ DRIZZLE. It sounds like you've had an interesting week, Mih My! You're hanging in there, though. You might need to ask the good folks for some blessed oil to get through the rest of this semester.

MS. MYRICK. I just might need to look into that!

DJ DRIZZLE. Alright, you know what time it is, bill time. You can catch Ms. Myrick for an hour each Sunday afternoon. Don't miss out, and with that, peace!

Session 4

[*WX-309 jingle plays.*]

DJ DRIZZLE. What's good in the Dirty, Dirty?! We're back on with Mih My. Hey, Ms. Myrick.

MS. MYRICK. Hey there! You ain't happy to hear from me. You just wanna hear these stories. Go ahead and play the song so the people can get situated.

DJ DRIZZLE. You heard what she said, let's see what Jeremih cooking up in the studio with "Don't Tell 'Em."

[*DJ Drizzle plays "Don't Tell 'Em."*]

DJ DRIZZLE. [*Fades out "Don't Tell 'Em."*] Man, I don't even want to waste no time, what's good with these kids?

MS. MYRICK. An interesting argument happened Monday. The Haitians, Jamaicans, and Mexicans were going back and forth bickering. It was getting rather annoying, so

I tuned in so I could essentially calm them down.

> Student A: (American) "Y'all need to swim back over the border, the same way you came in, stupid immigrant. You taking all the jobs. That's why my people have to work in the field right now."

> Student B and C: (Mexican and Haitian) "You're an immigrant too!"

> And then the other "Americans" snapped on the boy who made the comment and said, "Boy, you so stupid, we all immigrants. We came from Africa, and we live on stolen land!"

> Student D: "You better not let *That's So Raven* fool you. We black, and we from Africa, 'cause everybody came from somewhere else. America don't have no real culture anyway."

So, I'm reaching for my little popcorn, and finally, I step in and say, "Get back to work, and stop making rude comments!"

DJ DRIZZLE. Those kids were getting tight. You were dancing around a physical altercation.

MS. MYRICK. I like when my students work out their problems without me having to jump in. I was jumping for joy on the inside because they are practicing all their reading strategies: drawing conclusions, making inferences, compare and contrast, etc. It was a good day in my classroom! But I also think it's time for me to incorporate a multicultural lesson before they kill each other about who is more American than who.

DJ DRIZZLE. I think so too! Ms. Myrick, rumor has it you have some surprising news coming our way. Is that true?

MS. MYRICK. Well yes, I do, but I think we should cue a song up so I can tell you the news and a couple of stories. What you think?

DJ DRIZZLE. I think you're trying to school me on this radio business, but I think you're right, so "Believe Me" by Lil Wayne will do.

[*DJ Drizzle plays "Believe Me."*]

DJ DRIZZLE. [*Fades out "Believe Me."*] I'm anxious over here, what's going on with you?

MS. MYRICK. Patience is a virtue! Let me tell you what this kid asked me on Thursday, though.

> Student A: "Ms. Myrick, I have a question."

> Me: "What's that?"

> Student A: "Is cannabis legal in Canada or something? Why is it on their country's flag?"

After crying of laughter, I had to explain it was a maple tree leaf because of the large amount of maple trees there. I think that's right. If not, it is way better than him thinking Canada promotes smoking weed.

DJ DRIZZLE. I didn't even know that; you have to be quick on your feet. So now can you tell everybody what's going on?

MS. MYRICK. Nope, I'll give you one more story. I can barely put my bags down, and here comes one of my favorites. It's middle school so, I just knew he came to school high. In fact, he was coming to get some work because they were sending him home the entire day for obvious reasons.

DJ DRIZZLE. What he say?

MS. MYRICK. Student A: "Ms., Phineas and Ferb been on summer vacation for ten years, when are they going back to school?"

> Me: "I'm sure they'll be getting off vacation the same time as you."

> Student A: "You ain't even have to do me like that."

> Me: "Get this work and get your life together."

DJ DRIZZLE. Yo, you are reckless with the kids. I did not know they've starting smoking at such a young age. That's new. Something tells me you told this story on purpose, so you'd have extra time to make us wait on the big news.

MS. MYRICK. You might be right.

DJ DRIZZLE. You heard Mih My. She's playing around with the news. Check out this "Na Na" from Trey Songz.

[*DJ Drizzle plays "Na Na."*]

DJ DRIZZLE. [*Fades out "Na Na."*] Na, you can't run from this news now, so out with it.

MS. MYRICK. Alright, so I'm leaving the middle school because my family needs my immediate attention at home. When it rains, it pours. My mom just found out she has Lupus and my dad literally just received some life-changing news that will affect him financially. So, with all of that, I will be moving back home to Atlanta. I've been secretly having interviews throughout the semester, and I'll be teaching in an elementary school.

DJ DRIZZLE. Wow! That's a jump. I think everybody wants to know what about the stories. Did you tell the kids?

MS. MYRICK. Well, I will continue to tell the stories, no worries. I did tell the kids the other day, and they weren't very happy. However, they were a lot more understanding than I thought. They gave me letters and hugs. My heart was full, and I will honor them for all the lessons they've taught me along the way. I can truly say, I love them, and I will miss them. Thinking about them is making me miss them like crazy!

DJ DRIZZLE. I can only imagine. I miss them too. Y'all don't understand, all the stories that go on in the middle school don't make it to the radio circuit. I'm just as attached to the kids as Mih My. Man, this news is devastating, but I'm sure Mih My will keep the stories flowing. With that said, you know the deal, let's pay these bills.

Session 5

[WX-309 jingle plays.]

DJ DRIZZLE. How y'all doing today?! I hope you all are having a blessed Sunday because I'm about to bless you with some new jams. Seems like a stranger called in. We'll be meeting this stranger a little later. Let's see what they have going on over in the west with "L.A.Love" by Fergie.

[DJ Drizzle plays "L.A.Love."]

DJ DRIZZLE. *[Fades out "L.A.Love."]* It's Casper y'all!

MS. MYRICK. Don't do that.

DJ DRIZZLE. Guess who's back. Uh-hum, back again.

MS. MYRICK. Drizzle, you just let me know when you're done selling out.

DJ DRIZZLE. Aight, I'm done, I'm done. How you been big time?!

MS. MYRICK. I'm just trying to be like you fam. But I'm back in Atlanta teaching in the county that raised me. I had a lovely welcome back home. The past two weeks have been extremely interesting. I teach little kids now, so I have to take them to the restroom. This is a big headache because the boys like to play in the restroom, see who can aim the furthest, and also pee on walls, etc. *I put an end to that.* So anytime I see or hear them making too much noise I have them leave.

DJ DRIZZLE. Please tell me it's a story involved.

MS. MYRICK. In this case, Student A decided to play a ninja in the restroom with his friend thinking I was not aware of what was going on, so this is where the story starts,

> Me: "Student A, you don't have to use the restroom?"
>
> Student A: "No."
>
> Me: "So, get out the restroom."

We leave and go back to class, and as soon as we are back in the classroom,

Student A: "Ms. Myrick, I have to use the restroom."

Me: (I'm livid.) "Wait five minutes until the class next door finishes, and I will send you."

DJ Drizzle, this little joker has a massive tantrum. He's screaming and kicking the desk, and I'm literally shocked because I must be in the twilight zone. Maybe two minutes passed,

Student A: "May I go to the nurse?"

Meanwhile, all the other kids say, "Ew, it's stinky."

Me: "Did you use the restroom?"

Student A: "Yes."

Me: "Why?"

Student A: "I was mad."

Me: "So, you chose to get embarrassed because you could not

wait for the other students to use the restroom. Now you're in trouble with your parents."

DJ DRIZZLE. Yo, that's wild. What did his mom say?

MS. MYRICK. Luckily, mommy came, and I was able to have a conference. Student A left crying. So, I win!

DJ DRIZZLE. Hahaha. I bet you hit your own Nae Nae, because you didn't have to deal with a crazy parent.

MS. MYRICK. You're right, but aye DJ, play that one time.

DJ DRIZZLE. Aight here's "Watch Me (Whip/Nae Nae)" by Silentó.

[*DJ Drizzle plays "Watch Me (Whip/Nae Nae)."*]

DJ DRIZZLE. [*Fades out "Watch Me (Whip/Nae Nae)."*] Yo Mih My, so what's the craziest thing to happen since you've been back in the A?

MS. MYRICK. Well, a parent and the grandparents came up to the school to address this little kid that is angry. On my third day, he ripped down all the posters in the class, and he's been a nightmare since. So, I was caught off guard because mom had a trail of tattoos coming from her eyes to her lips—I'd never seen that. I normally ask what influences tattoos, but I didn't. She was extremely supportive of her son, and that's all that mattered in my book.

DJ DRIZZLE. So, you've been calling parents every day, huh?

MS. MYRICK. If they send their child to school and he or she is continuously bothersome and violent with other student, I will contact that parent every hour on the hour until I see them, or changes are made.

DJ DRIZZLE. And there you have it. I'd hate to be on the other side of that phone call. But we're out of time. We're so glad to have Casper back with us, but let's pay these bills y'all. Peace.

Session 6

[WX-309 jingle plays.]

DJ DRIZZLE. What's good in the Dirty, Dirty?! We're back on with Mih My. Hey, Ms. Myrick. I don't know if I can keep inviting you back because these kids are out of order.

MS. MYRICK. Hey there. Now you know you want to hear these stories. Stop playing! [Inserts laugh] I think you should play the new Rihanna and Kanye song first.

DJ DRIZZLE. You heard what she said, let's see what Rihanna and Kanye's cooking up in the studio with "FourFiveSeconds."

[DJ Drizzle plays "FourFiveSeconds."]

DJ DRIZZLE. *[Fades out "FourFiveSeconds."]* We're back. I'm on air with Ms. Myrick if you're just tuning in. You're right on time because she is about to tell us what our favorite classroom comedians are up to.

MS. MYRICK. So, I've been having some of the best teaching days of my life, you hear me?! Lol. Every. Single. Day. But it's never a dull day with this bunch of kids. I am coming with a few stories.

DJ DRIZZLE. You seem happy about these stories.

MS. MYRICK. We're outside for our break, and the boys are playing a reckless version of football. You guys at the parks have to teach these jokers some technique with tackling. They look like they are ripping each other's neck off.

DJ DRIZZLE. That's my type of action.

MS. MYRICK. Anyway, the boys stop playing, and my Spidey senses kick in, so I'm paying close attention. The next line I hear is, "What the f***, you cheating n****?!" I clutch my imaginary pearls, and it starts to rain hard. So, I rush the kids inside the building and have a mini convo with the little guy. I ask why was he cussing like that, and he said 'cause they were getting on his nerves.

DJ DRIZZLE. He has to be listening to some folks at the house.

MS. MYRICK. Right? So, I ask does his people know he's cussing like that, and he said, "Yea, and they don't say anything about it." So, we called to check, just in case, and someone wasn't very happy.

DJ DRIZZLE. Uh-oh. He ain't getting a rain check for that discipline he's about to get at home.

MS. MYRICK. I said all that to say these kids are impressionable. So, we have to keep it Rated G because these jokers are cussing like sixty-five-year-old angry men playing chess or bingo or something.

DJ DRIZZLE. You know I have to work on that myself.

MS. MYRICK. I do as well because I know I can put some sentences together, but these kids are creative. I low-key feel ashamed taking notes!

DJ DRIZZLE. Now, Ms. Myrick.

MS. MYRICK. I have to keep it honest. Adults can use growth too. But check this out, it's time to go home, and I'm walking the kids to the bus, and a kid strikes up a conversation with a quiet kid in class.

Student A: "Why do you hate me?"

Student B: "It's three reasons I hate you: one, you're ignorant…"

DJ DRIZZLE. Yo, these kids are wild!

MS. MYRICK. It took the air out of my chest.

DJ DRIZZLE. Did you laugh, be honest?

MS. MYRICK. I have to save my laughter for something funnier.

DJ DRIZZLE. Did you have any good days?

MS. MYRICK. Oh yes, I was saving the best for last!

DJ DRIZZLE. Good, so what happened because you make it seem like these kids are tyrants.

MS. MYRICK. They can be, but on Friday, the superintendent walked inside my classroom, and my students gave him the business.

DJ DRIZZLE. Uh-oh, these kids about to get you fired?

MS. MYRICK. Check me out, they were working on a project that required them to make an aquarium out of a Styrofoam cup, and only invertebrates could be inside. So, after the most awkward introduction and the kids not knowing who the superintendent was at all, I started to ask them questions about invertebrates. Everybody was focused and attentive. I mean they went in definitions, descriptions, examples, showing the project.

DJ DRIZZLE. Oh, yea! That's what I'm talking about. I knew they would show up.

MS. MYRICK. They showed out! He walked out, and they said, "Ms. Myrick, are you proud of us? We didn't embarrass you, did we?!" I was extremely proud of them, but I can't stop being mean until Christmas, maybe. Lol.

DJ DRIZZLE. Now, you have to give them a piece of candy or something because this was a difficult task for them.

MS. MYRICK. Maybe close to Christmas, but I'm going to continue to praise them for their good effort and behavior to keep this momentum going.

DJ DRIZZLE. I'm glad you ended with a good story, but if I don't play another song, they are going to cut this radio station, and we're both going to be looking crazy! Lol.

MS. MYRICK. Well, let me pick the song.

DJ DRIZZLE. You got it, Ms. Myrick.

MS. MYRICK. You are listening to WX-309, the best radio station this side of the Mason Dixon Line. "Classic Man" is coming up next!

Session 7

[*WX-309 jingle plays.*]

DJ DRIZZLE. What's good in the Dirty, Dirty?! We're back on with Mih My. Hey, Ms. Myrick. The last time we had Ms. Myrick in the studio, she had a range of stories. Tell the people what's up!

MS. MYRICK. These kids are out of control.

DJ DRIZZLE. Before you start, let's get the people prepared with a little "March Madness" by Future.

[*DJ Drizzle plays "March Madness."*]

DJ DRIZZLE. [*Fades out "March Madness."*] You don't look as excited this week.

MS. MYRICK. Actually, I'm trying to figure out how to tell you the stories without laughing. But I'll start here.

DJ DRIZZLE. Okay, don't keep us waiting.

MS. MYRICK. I'm walking down the hallway, and I see my favorite sixty-something-year-old janitor.

DJ DRIZZLE. Wait a minute. You're supposed to be talking about the kids.

MS. MYRICK. Are you going to let me tell or what?

DJ DRIZZLE. Don't get this man divorced!

MS. MYRICK. This is how it went,

> Janitor: "How you doing, ma'am?"

> Me: "I'm okay, I'm tired. I can't wait to go home and go to sleep."

> Janitor: "I been sleep all damn weekend; you would have thought I was pregnant."

> Me: "Lol."
> Janitor: "I'm saying, ma'am, my wife asked me if I was pregnant and I said, 'Well if I am, you did it!'"

> Me: "Lol."

DJ DRIZZLE. Whomp, whomp, whomp. That wasn't funny.

MS. MYRICK. Well, I needed that pick me up because these kids were acting up.

DJ DRIZZLE. Okay, tell us about it.

MS. MYRICK. The kids had to read their children's book project.

DJ DRIZZLE. Oh, Ms. Myrick, you trippin'. You got these kids writing children's books?

MS. MYRICK. Hold up, watch your mouth. I have to make these kids be ten times better than the other kids who get the resources they don't have. If I don't push them, no one will.

DJ DRIZZLE. Did you fuss at me a little bit?

MS. MYRICK. And I did…now listen. One student brought "wolf teeth" to make her presentation spectacular. As she's reading the story, she puts the wolf teeth in her mouth for speaking parts.

> Student A: "Ms. Myrick, my grandma got some teef like that for real."

> Me: "Lol."

> Student: "I ain't lying. Hers a little smaller though, and she put dat mint stuff on it too. She wear them on the bottom like this."

DJ DRIZZLE. No!

MS. MYRICK. It gets better. So, I asked, "What are these teeth called?"

> Half of the class screams, "Dem grandma teef!"
> "Nuh-uh, dem replacement teef!"
> "Eww, yo grandma, don't brush ha tooth. She put it in dat water, she nasty!"

DJ DRIZZLE. Y'all…I'm. In. Real. Tears!

MS. MYRICK. Yo, I'm trying to gather my composure and as they were switching classes, one of the sweetest students, genuinely concerned, asked, "Ms. Myrick, do your momma got teef?!"

DJ DRIZZLE. What you going to do with those kids?

MS. MYRICK. I'm stuck for another semester, so I'm not certain, but if I could give them back early, trust me, I would!

DJ DRIZZLE. But how are we going to laugh?

MS. MYRICK. It wouldn't be so bad but, they start their shenanigans so early in the morning, at seven a.m. Check this out, this little boy was creeping up on me this morning. As I was trying to avoid him, he says, "Aye, Ms. Myrick, I'm messed up this morning. My momma got me in this uniform, she ain't let me go to my grandma's house to get my shoes, and then last night something was chasing me in the kitchen, and then I turned around, and I screamed, 'Momma, help me!'"

DJ DRIZZLE. Wait. What?

MS. MYRICK. Student, "You know what she gon tell me? She told me to go to sleep, and I'm out here dyin' bruh. She be trippin'."

DJ DRIZZLE. All that at seven in the morning?

MS. MYRICK. Then immediately after I had a parent call me. She had the audacity to tell me I need to stop giving her child homework every day. I just looked at the phone. I think we were both afraid of what was about to come out my mouth next. I give one sheet of paper for homework, to color, are you kidding me?!

DJ DRIZZLE. You just gave them a book to do.

MS. MYRICK. That's different, and they had a month to do that project.

DJ DRIZZLE. I guess you're right.

MS. MYRICK. This time, I am. Now play the music before you get fussed at too!

Session 8

[*WX-309 jingle plays.*]

DJ DRIZZLE. How y'all doing today?! You're listening to WX-309, and I'm almost afraid to have Ms. Myrick come on because she almost snapped on me the last time.

MS. MYRICK. That's right! You didn't have my back on coloring a sheet of paper! It's your own people.

DJ DRIZZLE. Before I let you finish snapping on me, can I please pay the bills?

MS. MYRICK. Go ahead.

DJ DRIZZLE. Coming up, we have "The Hills" by The Weeknd.

[*DJ Drizzle plays "The Hills."*]

DJ DRIZZLE. [*Fades out "The Hills."*] Ms. Myrick is my friend again y'all. I sent her money for snacks.

MS. MYRICK. Okay, but why you so loud?

DJ DRIZZLE. I obviously didn't send enough money [*Inserts obnoxious laugh*].

MS. MYRICK. Anyway, y'all men always cutting up.

DJ DRIZZLE. What you mean?

MS. MYRICK.

> *To whom this may concern:*
>
> *Please be sure to dispose of your old cell phone pictures prior to giving it to your nine or ten-year-old child, because they may be sitting in the back of the class looking at you and someone else "having fun." The walk of shame is never fun, especially when it's to get the phone from your child's school. Lol.*
>
> *Sincerely,*
>
> *Your child's teacher for about seven more months.*

DJ DRIZZLE. I know you lying!

MS. MYRICK. No, I'm not. It's crazy because, well, it was an entanglement.

DJ DRIZZLE. Entanglement?

MS. MYRICK. It was complicated.
Everybody in the house was embarrassed.

DJ DRIZZLE. I'm speechless.

MS. MYRICK. I told you. Y'all men.

DJ DRIZZLE. That's just reckless, but I still
believe black men don't cheat!

MS. MYRICK. Anyway, so last Tuesday, the
kids came from Spanish and were unusually
chatty.

DJ DRIZZLE. That's not unusual.

MS. MYRICK. I have a new student from up
north, and he's trying to get adjusted to the
southern drawl.

> New kid: "Ms. Myrick, why do they
> keep saying 'bra'?"

> MS. MYRICK. "Lol."

> Student A: "Bruh."

> New Kid: "It's like bruuaaaa? What's
> it even mean? What's it mean?"

Student B: "No, bruh. Dang."

MS. MYRICK. At this point, I'm weak 'cause I can't get the answer out.

> Student C: "You know we can't say bruh in Spanish class 'cause the teacher don't like it. She said, 'You don't say Brrrraaaaa, braaaaaaa (singing BRA in a high pitch voice) in here again!' Lol."

DJ DRIZZLE. So, they still don't know Spanish because they were stuck on saying bruh?

MS. MYRICK. Precisely.

DJ DRIZZLE. Do they act up in specials all the time?

MS. MYRICK. Yes, but they give us a break sometimes. So, in music, they hate music.

DJ DRIZZLE. What happened now?

MS. MYRICK. Well, I pronounce "again" like "a-gain,"

> Student A: "You know you say again, just like the music teacher?"

The most annoying kid ever patiently waiting to be answered. I finally acknowledge him to answer his question.

> Student B: "Is the music teacher special?"

> Me: "Special?"

> Student A: "Like, slow?"

> Me: "Well, no. He is not more special than you."

DJ DRIZZLE. That man has a whole degree, and did you just call that boy slow?

MS. MYRICK. Look, you have to be quick. If you don't have a plan for them, they will have a plan for you.

DJ DRIZZLE. Well, did they learn anything this week?

MS. MYRICK. Oh, they learn every week, don't try and play me. I have receipts.

DJ DRIZZLE. Receipts!

MS. MYRICK. I'll bring my data in here, and your jaw will hit the flow. I'm not cocky, but I'm pretty much the greatest of all time in *my* classroom.

DJ DRIZZLE. Well, excuse me.

MS. MYRICK. Well, since we are here, during math centers, one of my students started to vent,

> Student A: "Ms. Myrick, I had to go sleep with my momma last night. You want to know why?"

> Me: "Actually, I don't."

> Student A: "I keep dying in my dreams. I got shot to death one day, I got stabbed to death another day, but I always wake up when I die. I be scared."

> Me: "You want to go to the counselor?"

DJ DRIZZLE. So, you just going to send that boy to the counselor while he is vulnerable?

MS. MYRICK. Look that is above my pay grade, and we have to report that kind of stuff. You interrupted me!

DJ DRIZZLE. Oops, my bad.

MS. MYRICK. This boy going to tell me, "Nah, I just wanted to tell you. I think I keep dying 'cause I do your math homework right before I go to sleep."

DJ DRIZZLE. This the second week in a row, we have homework complaints. I'm starting to think it is you.

MS. MYRICK. Math is difficult. They will always complain. The more they practice, the better they will be. This student is just dramatic.

DJ DRIZZLE. I don't know now, let's see what happens next week because you may be low-key torturing those kids.

MS. MYRICK. I'm going to go ahead and introduce the next song before y'all favorite DJ gets on my bad side. Up next is "Here" by Alessia Cara because I'm still wondering why I'm here.

DJ DRIZZLE. Wow!

Session 9

[*WX-309 jingle plays.*]

DJ DRIZZLE. How y'all doing today?! You're listening to WX-309, and I have my best buddy in the Dirty South hanging with me today.

MS. MYRICK. Don't butter me up, you still ain't worth two dead flies.

DJ DRIZZLE. Look, I'm going to play "Hello" by Adele, so besties can learn how to properly greet people.

MS. MYRICK. Ha, I see you learned a lesson or two from the last session.

[*DJ Drizzle plays "Hello."*]

DJ DRIZZLE. [*Fades out "Hello."*] And we're back with the biggest hater in Decatur.

MS. MYRICK. Here you go, leading me right into my story on harmful and beneficial. Your commentary is not beneficial right now.

DJ DRIZZLE. Can we just start over?

MS. MYRICK. Yes. Let's. Go ahead, say sorry.

DJ DRIZZLE. Good evening, Ms. Myrick, how are you?

MS. MYRICK. Much better, thank you for asking.

DJ DRIZZLE. What's going on with the kids?

MS. MYRICK. So last week, we were discussing harmful and beneficial cells, and we'd come upon the vocabulary word "infectious disease." The sentence in the book says, "Viral diseases such as hepatitis and AIDS have killed many people."

DJ DRIZZLE. This about to take a sharp turn.

MS. MYRICK. You're right.

> Student A: "Ms. Myrick, what's AIDS?"

> Me: "It's a viral disease that attacks your immune system."

> Student B: "Eazy E had that, ain't he?"

Me: "Yes."

Student B: "Man, ew, that's 'cause he kept doing, you know what," as he points to his private area.

Student C: "Is that the disease that turns you into a zombie?"

DJ DRIZZLE. Jesus, take the wheel!

MS. MYRICK. It wasn't exactly wrong.

DJ DRIZZLE. Did you answer back?

MS. MYRICK. No, I told him to finish taking his Cornell Notes, and the answer will be in the next question.

DJ DRIZZLE. You getting slow with the clap back.

MS. MYRICK. No, you just have to pick and choose your battles. Plus, they just want to be off task so bad.

DJ DRIZZLE. You're going to have an extra pearl in your crown when you go to heaven.

MS. MYRICK. You're right. I'm tired, though.

DJ DRIZZLE. Tell me about it.

MS. MYRICK. We don't get a fall break, so I have to check my emotions and the kids too.

DJ DRIZZLE. Tell me about the kids because I don't want to hear you complaining about your master's program. You chose that torture.

MS. MYRICK. See, you love to dig a hole for yourself.

DJ DRIZZLE. My bad, give me another chance.

MS. MYRICK. Anyway, a kid meets me at the door with a little tear in his eye,

> Student A: "Ms. Myrick, this is frustrating!"

> Me: "Okay."

> Student A: "My momma mad at me for some reason. I got my shoes taken, and I got this ugly haircut. My momma ain't even like this haircut. Bruh at the shop going to cut my hair off. He just do what he want to do. He be trying to act like my daddy. He just like my momma, and she still messing with my sorry

daddy. It's just too much going on right now. I feel like Peter Parker. I got to be two people. This haircut sucks. It makes my head look big. This haircut look better on him than me. This haircut played out. I can't do this. Ms. Myrick, you have to help me. Tell my momma I had a fantastic day, so I don't have to wear these ugly shoes."

Me: "Is that all?"

Student A: "What did I do to deserve this?"

Me: "Leave me alone."

DJ DRIZZLE. Aye, why you do that man like that? That's why men grow up and don't express themselves because you shut him down.

MS. MYRICK. That may be right. I'm going to check myself. I just don't be having the energy.

DJ DRIZZLE. Well, find some because as much as you're tired, it seems like the kids enjoy you. Go to sleep early, you ain't got no kids.

MS. MYRICK. What we not going to do is act like I don't have a life outside of school.

DJ DRIZZLE. So, you dating?

MS. MYRICK. Mind your business, and no, but I can't come in here preaching to the kids about turning in quality work, and I'm being mediocre.

DJ DRIZZLE. These kids don't care what you have going on.

MS. MYRICK. Lie again. They are always trying to put me on with their uncle. They show me pictures of him at church and everything.

DJ DRIZZLE. For real, what can you do to be more available? I know you're tired but…

MS. MYRICK. I'll take two mental health days and take a trip to Florida to handle my "business."

DJ DRIZZLE. Oh, yea?

MS. MYRICK. Yes, but I appreciate that honesty, though. I'm still a young teacher, and I'm learning every day. It's hard teaching African American boys sometimes. They have so   much going against them.

Unfortunately, that's all we teach. I want to be better. I learned while teaching in Florida that I have to check my own privilege. Now, I have to teach ten-year-old boys how to function in their own privilege on top of teaching them that vulnerability isn't weak. No, it's not my job, but they learn more than just math and science in my class. It's either I teach them inside this classroom, or they learn from the streets.

DJ DRIZZLE. That's deep.

MS. MYRICK. Right? It's never too late to start setting positive examples.

DJ DRIZZLE. This was a pretty dope session, but we ran out of time!

MS. MYRICK. How about I tell this story to introduce the next song.

DJ DRIZZLE. Let me see what you got.

MS. MYRICK. I was dismissing my first block, and the new kid from up north asks, "Ms. Myrick, how come in the rap videos, they say chew, instead of you? They say, 'I don't mess with chheeeeeewwww (singing).'"

DJ DRIZZLE. You got jokes!

MS. MYRICK. You're listening to WX-309, and up next, we have Big Sean with "I Don't Mess with Cheeewwwwwww."

Session 10

[WX-309 jingle plays.]

DJ DRIZZLE. It's Sunday afternoon, and you know what that means, I have the best teacher here with me. I know y'all can't wait to hear from her. I'm excited this week. What about y'all?

MS. MYRICK. You don't know the half of it!

DJ DRIZZLE. Before we dig in, let's pay these bills!

MS. MYRICK. Yo, play "Hotline Bling."

DJ DRIZZLE. I love a woman that knows what she wants?

MS. MYRICK. Chill.

DJ DRIZZLE. *[Laughs hysterically and plays "Hotline Bling."]*

DJ DRIZZLE. *[Fades out "Hotline Bling."]* What's up, Ms. Myrick?

MS. MYRICK. Yo.

DJ DRIZZLE. The kids must be keeping you hip?

MS. MYRICK. They might be!

DJ DRIZZLE. What are my buddies up to now? At this point, do they know you talk about them every week?

MS. MYRICK. Kind of. I tell them they are going to make me rich someday.

DJ DRIZZLE. That may be true, claim it.

MS. MYRICK. We have this unstructured break time.

DJ DRIZZLE. Unstructured what?

MS. MYRICK. Recess.

DJ DRIZZLE. You could have just led with that.

MS. MYRICK. Hush, so listen. I'm watching the kids play so they don't kill each other, and I notice kids dancing, whipping the Nae Nae, all of that. Then, I see kids running toward me. The whole time I'm thinking, please go away, go play, ugh what do they want?!

Student A: (Out of breath.) "Ms. Myrick, we just had a funeral for this bug that Student B killed. We made up a song and dance."

Me: "Well, go kill another one, so I can see it."

The kids run back to have a ratchet version of praise and worship, and then one of the boys props up his leg to start twerking.

DJ DRIZZLE. Oh no.

MS. MYRICK. Wait, that's not the joke. A voice from around the corner says, "Look at ole Magic Mike!"

DJ DRIZZLE. I'm officially dead to the bed! How do you still have a job?

MS. MYRICK. I started to ask questions, but remember…

DJ DRIZZLE. Choose your battles.

MS. MYRICK. See you listen. Academically, it's even worse. I'm moving through the curriculum and introduce heredity and traits.

DJ DRIZZLE. This is going to be good.

MS. MYRICK. So, I'm breaking down one of the vocabulary words, "gene."

> Student A: "My momma skinny and my daddy fat, he in Jamaica, though."

> Student B: "So that's why you chubby 'cause it's in your genes, right Ms. Myrick? It ain't no such thing as big bones."

DJ DRIZZLE. They missed it.

MS. MYRICK. Let's just say I have a bit of re-teaching to do. That's not it; another student wouldn't stop talking.

DJ DRIZZLE. Well, that's nothing new.

MS. MYRICK. I say, "Please stop talking to me."

> Student A: "But Ms. Myrick, I can't help it. I can't control it, because it's an acquired gene, I was born with it. You just taught me that, see."

> Me: "I'm about to get your mother on the phone, so you can talk her to death."

Student A: "Okay, okay. I'll chill."

DJ DRIZZLE. I feel like they know, they just want to play.

MS. MYRICK. Of course, they know.

DJ DRIZZLE. You going to let them have a fall harvest party?

MS. MYRICK. We only get to have two parties a year because it is a disruption to the school day, so we don't have extra birthdays, kwanza, bar mitzvah…in Florida, yes, but Georgia, no.

DJ DRIZZLE. Being a kid sucks now. Elementary school was fire when we were younger.

MS. MYRICK. I remember having fun. Trust, they want one. Thursday, this kid was staring into space. I said, "What are you looking at?"

Student A: "I'm just happy. Thanksgiving is like Christmas for me."

Me: "Why?"

Student A: "Cause I got me a girlfriend, and my grandma cleaned five buckets of chitlins that Imma eat when I get home, and we got some pig feet and pig ears too."

Student B: "Boy, you ain't got no girlfriend. I bet she fat if you do."

Student A: "She is real. She in middle school. She fine too."

Student C: "You still nasty 'cause you eat pig feet, pig ears, and pig boo boo. And you too short to have a girlfriend."

Me: "Okay, I'm over it. Be quiet."

DJ DRIZZLE. You walked right into that!

MS. MYRICK. I was practicing being available to kids, remember?

DJ DRIZZLE. Nah, this is not a good example.

MS. MYRICK. Was I reaching for that one?

DJ DRIZZLE. Yea.

Ms. Myrick. Did I ever tell you I have a co-teacher?

DJ Drizzle. No, what's that. Like a teacher aid?

Ms. Myrick. No, they are real teachers that serve students with learning disabilities.

DJ Drizzle. Y'all teach at the same time?

Ms. Myrick. Not exactly, but we use a model that the kids are comfortable with.

DJ Drizzle. So, you teach "special education?"

Ms. Myrick. It's called "exceptional education" now.

DJ Drizzle. Well, teach me, teacher.

Ms. Myrick. Learn something new every day. So, my fourth block was interrupted with, "Leave me alone."

> Co-Teacher: "What's going on?"

> Student A: "He keeps asking me what time I go to church."

> Co-Teacher: "Come here."

(Student B walks over.)
Student B: "He just acting like a baby."

Co-Teacher: "Why are you asking him what time he goes to church?"

Student B: "Cause he keep saying he go to church. He don't act like it, so I was just asking him what time."

DJ DRIZZLE. So, you just not going to say nothing?

MS. MYRICK. Absolutely not, she can handle it. Meanwhile, Student A in the background humming.

DJ DRIZZLE. This doesn't sound like a good ending.

MS. MYRICK. "I'm almost positive I said be quiet, what's that noise?!"

Class: "Student A singing."

Student A: "I'm just singing a gospel song."

Me: "So, you're trying to prove you go to church by singing?"

Co-Teacher: "Sing it out loud."

Student A: (Insert vibrato and bounce rock back and forth.) "VICTORY IS MINE, VICTORY IS MINE."

DJ DRIZZLE. No buddy didn't.

MS. MYRICK. Oh yes, he did, and every time someone opened the door, I had him put on a concert.

DJ DRIZZLE. You enjoyed every bit of that, huh?

MS. MYRICK. The student did too.

DJ DRIZZLE. Did this happen in math or science?

MS. MYRICK. That was math. Now science was a whole different conversation.

DJ DRIZZLE. I'm all in now, what happened?

Ms. Myrick. The boys were upset that I was teaching them about reproduction,

Student A: "Why you have to teach us about sexual reproduction?"

Me: "Because the state is requiring me too. Plus, you're of age to know where babies come from."

Student B: "Well, I already know. Babies come from God. See, you ask God for a boy or a girl, God gives you what you want in your stomach, and there you have it."

Student C: "Nuh-uh. Babies just pop out, and if you don't catch it, they die."

Me: (Face palm.)

Student D: "They come out of a hole. You just dig them up and boom, there you have it—a baby. That's what my momma said."

> Me: "Lol, is that right?! You're in for the surprise of your life."

> Concerned Student E (Girl): "Do babies really come from the sky?"

DJ DRIZZLE. The sky?

MS. MYRICK. Of all the things they said, you chose the comment about the sky?

DJ DRIZZLE. Please tell me you broke it down?

MS. MYRICK. If I tell you what I said, you're going to have to pay me.

DJ DRIZZLE. Can we at least end on a good note?

MS. MYRICK. Well, my kids love to show off things they learn in other classes. So, I was giving my third block a test,

> Me: "I need you to take your test. Wait! Never mind. You'll only have ten minutes before specials, so wait until after gym to take it."

> Student A: "Opportunity Cost."

Me: "But, you have to go to gym!"

Student A: "Well, I'm going to give up gym to take my test. It's more important."

Me: "I won't fight you on it. Go ahead."

DJ DRIZZLE. So, he skipped something fun for a test?

MS. MYRICK. Yes! That and he used what he was learning in social studies and made a real-life connection. That's what it's all about.

DJ DRIZZLE. You're right, and that's it for our session. We are way over the time. You're listening to WX-309, the finest station in the Dirty South. Check us out next week. You don't want to miss it!

Session 11

[*WX-309 jingle plays.*]

DJ DRIZZLE. It's Sunday afternoon, and you know what that means, we are spreading the jams and chilling with our favorite teacher. It's almost time for winter break. I know you're excited.

MS. MYRICK. You don't know the half of it!

DJ DRIZZLE. Before we dig into the juicy stories, let's take it back one time.

MS. MYRICK. Can you please play "My Boo" with Usher and Alicia Keys?

DJ DRIZZLE. You in your feelings, huh?

MS. MYRICK. Chill.

DJ DRIZZLE. [*Laughs hysterically*] Just for you. [*Plays "My Boo."*]

DJ DRIZZLE. [*Fades out "My Boo."*] And just like that, we're back. So Mih My, what's going on with you in the A? Is it true all the kids talk like Offset from the Migos?

Ms. Myrick. [*Laughs*] I see you got jokes. But no, they don't. They sound more like Quavo.

DJ Drizzle. You're shot out! Man, tell us about the kids and stop playing so much.

Ms. Myrick. It's not too much happening. They're losing their minds. Christmas is around the corner, so their brain cells are fried. I was trying to teach them to tell time, and the kids said, "Ms. Myrick, it's eight o ten!"

DJ Drizzle. Word?!

Ms. Myrick. Jesus, take the wheel! They have intense conversations. Yesterday, the kids had an argument about if Santa was real or not. They even started to cry. Remember when we had these kinds of problems? Now, the worldly issues we face now are just crazy, don't you think? Hmm.

DJ Drizzle. I wish I could go back. Those were the good ole days! Did you tell them the truth?

Ms. Myrick. I was enjoying the debate, and honestly, I didn't want to take away from their imagination.

DJ DRIZZLE. So now that you're probably at your wit's end. How are you feeling about the parental involvement?

MS. MYRICK. [*Clears throat*] I just feel like a bunch of parents are breaking the law. I believe if I dig deep enough in one of my education books or maybe even Google, there is a law that states, and don't quote me, that every child is granted a free, equal, and quality education. That's a law somewhere, I know it. Now parents that send unruly kids have produced kids that do not know how to act, and therefore they are prohibiting other students to an equal, and quality education because they are disrupting quality instruction, which means they are breaking the law. Ultimately, the parents are breaking the law because they knew what type of child left their house and allowed it to happen. Somebody needs to go to jail. I know I'm reaching, but something has to give! Lol. It's been a long month.

DJ DRIZZLE. You are not pleased.

MS. MYRICK. It's just so frustrating. Teachers wear many hats. We don't get a chance to choose teaching as just our only occupation. This profession is not like other professions where you are expected to complete one specific task. Teachers are counselors, doctors, nurses, computer engineers, and many more. When we don't have any parental support, it adds to our list of things to combat in what seems to be a constant war zone. Teachers are literally going through PTSD, and I'm sure they know it.

DJ DRIZZLE. Well, I wasn't expecting that! I'm not sure that people understand the severity of this occupation.

MS. MYRICK. I think people equate teaching as a regular occupation sometimes. They expect us to say, "Do you want fries with that?" Or maybe, "You can have it your way." I'm not certain that the community understands the dynamics of teaching, and I'm not sure that teachers do a good job of explaining those dynamics.

DJ DRIZZLE. Do you honestly think they care?

MS. MYRICK. Depends on the demographic.

DJ DRIZZLE. I'd love to continue this conversation with you, but the people want to know about the kids too. What are they up to these days?

MS. MYRICK. Of course, well,

> Student A: "Ms. Mygrit," (Just because they can't say my name.) "he said the S-word."

> Me: (Rolls eyes, thinking I wish y'all would shut up but, which S-word is it this time.) "What S-word?"

> Student A: "Sexy."

> Student B: (Yelling at the top of their lungs.) "Nuh-uh. She asked me why my parents not together and I said cause my mommy said that my daddy was sexy with other women, and I told her she don't need to ask about that 'cause my momma said it ain't nobody business what happens in our house."

> Student A: "No, I didn't." (Starts crying.)

MS. MYRICK. [*Face palm*] Is it one fifty yet?

DJ DRIZZLE. That's a pretty invasive story. How do you approach something like that?

MS. MYRICK. I normally don't tell the parents, but I do ask them to re-route their thoughts, so the conversation isn't as inappropriate. I think I know more about the parents' personals than they do. After all, they are still trying to grasp what their parents are talking about. They have an idea at this age that something happens, I'm just not comfortable with telling   them about the birds and the bees, whatever that means.

DJ DRIZZLE. You don't know the story of the birds and the bees?

MS. MYRICK. Absolutely not, I actually think it's a dumb metaphor to try to convey to children.

DJ DRIZZLE. I don't think I had the conversation either. I'm nervous, even thinking about how my parents would have portrayed the metaphor myself. What else happened this week?

MS. MYRICK. Thursday was just such a train wreck, but per request, I'll tell you about my angry tantrum kid. This tantrum was so epic, I couldn't do anything but laugh. Let me provide a little background. My students do not bring supplies. They only bring Nintendo games, new Kevin Durant sneakers, stuff like that. Pencils, paper, bookbags…ha, that's a joke. One of the students asked me for a pencil. I said no because the last time I gave you a brand-new pencil, you played karate with your friends and broke it.

(Begin tantrum) The student starts screaming, "I hate you, I hate this school," kicks trashcan over, falls over trashcan, gets angrier, pushes the boy that beat him up already, kicks desks, bites ashy lips, throws books out of desk...still screaming. The boy that crashes spaceships with his pencils all day says he is scared, and then he said, "When I ask for the pencil, you supposed to give me a pencil."

Now, Drizzle, this is when I had to make a decision: job versus no job. It was the end of the day, so I did not expect any help from administration. I walked him to the car, and his interesting weekend started in the car in which I was very pleased because he received what I almost gave him inside the class.

DJ DRIZZLE. What happened in the car?!

MS. MYRICK. Use your imagination! I haven't flipped a desk since I left Florida, but the old Ms. Myrick almost flew out. I just couldn't remember if my legal paperwork processed. Totally just kidding.

DJ DRIZZLE. I don't think you're joking.

MS. MYRICK. I learned to flip stuff over in high school. My director was angry the day before a big showcase against another school. Papers, a baton, cellphones, and earring backs flew everywhere.

DJ DRIZZLE. Well, teachers are your first teacher!

MS. MYRICK. I'd say parents, but for some, yes, teachers are.

DJ DRIZZLE. You might be right. Well, that's our time. I look forward to continuing this conversation about teachers and their value in the world next Sunday! As always, thank you, the lovely Mih My for all the

love. But you know the deal, let's pay these
bills. Peace.

Session 12

[*WX-309 jingle plays.*]

DJ DRIZZLE. What's good in the Dirty South?! We're back on with your favorite teacher and my favorite teacher, Ms. Myrick.

MS. MYRICK. Don't give me too much, I don't know how to act. I know you're not that happy to hear from me, you just wanna hear these stories.

DJ DRIZZLE. You know this time I'm actually happy to hear from you! To show you how much I care, I'm going to pay homage to a new hometown hero, Fetty Wap.

MS. MYRICK. If it isn't "679," I don't wanna hear it!

DJ DRIZZLE. Your wish is my command [*Plays "679"*].

DJ DRIZZLE. [*Fades out "679."*] So, you got those stories or what?

MS. MYRICK. You're feenin' for these stories, huh?

DJ DRIZZLE. Just tell the story, man.

MS. MYRICK. Tuesday of this week,

> Student A: "Where do babies come from?"
>
> Me: "Ask your mom."

Drizzle, I'm shaking in my boots. I think he's going to forget and come back the next day curious.

DJ DRIZZLE. How did you weasel yourself out of this one?

MS. MYRICK. It gets better. We're in class,

> Student A: "I asked my mom, and she said they come from your 'P-word,'" as he points down to his stomach.
>
> Me: (Long deep confused sigh)
> "Okay, so now you know."
>
> Student A: (He is still lingering around) "Well, what's a 'P-word?'"

> Me: "The P in 'P-word' stands for a woman's 'pouch.' You know it's almost the same as how the mothers of kangaroos hold their babies."

> Student A: "He says, 'Oh, okay!'"

Low-key, I was peeking out the corner of my eyes, hoping he wouldn't ask any more questions. He didn't! Did I save the day or what?! Lol, see had this been a different age group (much, much older) I probably would have told him, but I couldn't bring myself to do it. He is eight, Lol. I'm still trying to figure out why his mom said, "P-word," or if it slipped. Maybe she doesn't know what the parts of the body start with. I don't know. I'm still in awe. If it's the "P-word" I think she was about to say; then I'm just truly shaking my head.

DJ DRIZZLE. Parents, we have to do better than this! When is a good time to have that conversations? These kids are seven and eight years old. That's scary.

MS. MYRICK. I think the appropriate time is now. If you don't have these open and honest conversations now, then the streets will teach them the hard way.

DJ DRIZZLE. You're right.

MS. MYRICK. And not that you care, but I had to flex on them real quick and beat the boys at arm wrestling. They were embarrassed they got beat by one, a girl, and two, their teacher. They will probably go home and eat their Wheaties and do some arm curls to beat me   next month. Lol.

DJ DRIZZLE. Now, Ms. Myrick, you are too old.

MS. MYRICK. They keep me youthful!

DJ DRIZZLE. We are going to close out this evening. Thank you for always rocking with the neighborhood station WX-309. We will see you next time!

<u>Session 13</u>

[WX-309 jingle plays.]

DJ DRIZZLE. What's good in the Dirty South?! It's been a while, but we're back in action with a familiar face, Ms. Myrick, what have you been up to?

MS. MYRICK. The second semester is usually wild around elementary schools. You know I have to vent, and I know you're only using me for stories anyway.

DJ DRIZZLE. You heard what she said, but before we get it poppin' with Mih My, let's see what Young Thug has been doing in the studio with "Check."

[DJ Drizzle Plays "Check." Fades back into the studio.]

DJ DRIZZLE. What's going on with the kids?

MS. MYRICK. It's been strange. I'll catch you up a bit. Imagine the moment you're coming to school beaming because you know you're about to kill a lesson on life cycles. It's planned to perfection, and the unexpected happens. All is well until one curious kid asks, "So, do babies come from seeds too?!" I'm quick with a no, and I keep pushing until another kid jumps in and says, "Only girls can have babies."

DJ DRIZZLE. Oh no. Recover, recover!

MS. MYRICK. Well, I said, "No, a male seahorse can carry a child." They were shocked into silence, and my plan for teaching didn't crash.

DJ DRIZZLE. Why do you even know that?

MS. MYRICK. The Georgia Aquarium [laughs], but check this, I was getting an annual observation. It was a life or death situation, so I saved my job!

DJ DRIZZLE. Yea, you did, that was lightweight, give me some juiciness.

MS. MYRICK. Well, you know it's testing time. That is a long season for teachers. So, this particular day was just hell on wheels. Administration wanted the kids to be silent in the hallway. Well, for elementary school, specifically eight to ten-years-old, that is the worst idea to possibly think of, and then they were not able to have gym because the coach was proctoring a test. Needless to say, the kids ended up fighting.

DJ DRIZZLE. Yo, the kids were wildlin'?

MS. MYRICK. It was bad, the little guy was furious, he played duck duck goose on those kids' faces.

DJ DRIZZLE. Did you break it up?

MS. MYRICK. We're not allowed to break up fights, but I can tell you he was sick of their antics. Anyway, I call the mother of one of the victims, and she says, "Well, I guess he learned his lesson, huh?!"

DJ DRIZZLE. Oh, so the mom knew he was a tyrant.

MS. MYRICK. I could have just hit the floor laughing. But I kept my composure. I needed a strong beverage after that. Drizzle, honestly, I have three more days of this testing torture.

DJ DRIZZLE. You sure you want to do this?

MS. MYRICK. Better than working with adults! I have more to tell you. It's quick I promise.

DJ DRIZZLE. Now you know I have to pay the bills. Let's do a quick break and get back to it.

[*Takes Break.*]

DJ DRIZZLE. We're back, and Ms. Myrick is on the line. She's been dropping the juicy tales in the elementary school, and I have to say these kids are trippin'. She bringing us some bonus heat before she leaves us again.

MS. MYRICK. Don't do that. Yo, check me out, I was eavesdropping on the kids while working in a small group. You ready? So, this is how it went,

> Student A: "Aye, what's Martin Luther King plus Michael Jordan equal?"
>
> Student B: "It equals deez nuts plus your hairline got em."

DJ DRIZZLE. Wait that doesn't even make any sense?

MS. MYRICK. When you were in elementary school, did anything make sense? I don't think he knew what he said or that he's in trouble. That was just one table, so I take a quick glance around the room and one of my girls has on a cute dress and is bending over trying to get some materials.

DJ DRIZZLE. I know you helped her out.

MS. MYRICK. Yea, I said, "You aren't supposed to bend over in that dress like that, cross your feet like this," demonstrating a squat.

> Student A (Boy): "That's right cause you supposed to let a man bend you over."

DJ DRIZZLE. You're lying?

MS. MYRICK. I'm not, and before you ask, I was so in shock. I couldn't recover!

DJ DRIZZLE. It seems like these elementary school students are worse than middle school.

MS. MYRICK. You know what, I believe that with my whole heart.

DJ DRIZZLE. Ms. Myrick this has been the highlight of my week, and I'm happy to have you. We only have two more sessions, are you sad?

MS. MYRICK. Actually, the school year is coming to an end. So, yes, I'm happy, but you know I'm going to miss sharing these conversations with you.

DJ DRIZZLE. Let's just hope they keep it Rated G next time.

MS. MYRICK. Let's! DJ Drizzle go ahead and play "Flex" by Rich Homie.

DJ DRIZZLE. I like your style, Ms. Myrick. Until next time.

Session 14

[WX-309 jingle plays.]

DJ DRIZZLE. What's good in the Dirty South?! You're tuned in to the number one satellite radio station, where we keep you up to date with everything important. Today we have Ms. Myrick on the line, and she seems stressed. I'm going to hurry up and play this song so we can get right into it!

[DJ Drizzle Plays "She Knows" by Ne-Yo.]

DJ DRIZZLE. *[Fades out "She Knows."]* Ms. Myrick, what up?!

MS. MYRICK. Man, you know it's wild! I'll give you just two stories today. I'm still stressed!

DJ DRIZZLE. Alright, what's up?

MS. MYRICK. It's Field Day. Now you know it's hot and it gets poppin' on the field.

DJ DRIZZLE. Uh-oh.

MS. MYRICK. All seemed well until the boys had to race. Racing is how you earn your bragging rights in elementary school, well at least to my students.

> Student A: "You a b****."

> Student B: (Slaps Student A.)

> (Insert kids from other classes screaming, and my class just quietly watching).

DJ DRIZZLE. So, they scrapping?

MS. MYRICK. Drizzle, it's rough. I come across to tell them to stop because we can't touch them, and Student A is flying across two rows of chairs. Student B is now fighting for street cred.

DJ DRIZZLE. Yo, Ms. Myrick, you just letting these kids scrap?

MS. MYRICK. Man, yes. I wasn't about to get punched in the face.

DJ DRIZZLE. You crazy.

MS. MYRICK. But two male parents go and break up the fight. Student B swings again hitting somebody's daddy in the face.

DJ DRIZZLE. You mean to tell me the little boy beat up somebody daddy too?!

MS. MYRICK. That's exactly right.

DJ DRIZZLE. You know what, let me play Kendrick Lamar because you going to be alright.

[*DJ Drizzle Plays "Alright"*]

DJ DRIZZLE. [*Fades out "Alright"*] Y'all we back with Ms. Myrick, and she is telling us about Field Day and boy did they have a day. You alright, Ms. Myrick?

MS. MYRICK. Yes, I'm okay, but I'm counting down the days until it's time to get out of school. I promised you two more stories. You said one, but I'll give you two because these stories are so entertaining.

DJ DRIZZLE. Uh-oh, let's hear it.

MS. MYRICK. Today a student brought in some handcuffs, and a story followed.

DJ DRIZZLE. I know you're playing with me, Mih My!

MS. MYRICK. Why you never believe me? I'll just let your mind run wild with what he told.

DJ DRIZZLE. Don't do that!

MS. MYRICK. I will say this, my street-smart kid busts out saying, "Oh, I'm telling Ms. My. You being inappropriate because ya know adults use that in the...."

DJ DRIZZLE. Oh no!

MS. MYRICK. I gave that serious side-eye with the clenched teeth and said, "You better shut your mouth and dare not repeat it."

DJ DRIZZLE. You have to show me proof.

MS. MYRICK. You know what I knew you weren't going to believe me, so I took a picture.

DJ DRIZZLE. You never cease to amaze me.

MS. MYRICK. Okay. One more, one more, but this one is not funny.

DJ DRIZZLE. It can't get no worse than this.

MS. MYRICK. I took my kids to special area; they had gym this particular day. One of my sweet little babies came to me with something.

> Student A: "Ms. Myreaaaa, your student in trouble in the main office. He told this girl, 'That's why you suck your daddy d***.'"

MS. MYRICK. I'm not surprised at all. I corrected the tattle-tell about repeating it and proceeded to get seven more complaints.

DJ DRIZZLE. Where did he get that from? That's a wild statement!

MS. MYRICK. Right, but since he's in the front office, I assume they are following protocol. So, I get the kids settled, and the little boy comes back to class.

> Me: "Are you going home?"

> Student B: "No."

DJ DRIZZLE So, wait, he's not going home?

MS. MYRICK. I guess not. So, I didn't get into what was said in the front office, but I conferenced with him and told him about using foul language and choosing better words.

DJ DRIZZLE. Well, that's good you didn't fuss at him. You stayed calm. Kudos to you!

MS. MYRICK. Aht. Aht. Don't give me too much credit.

DJ DRIZZLE. What happened?

MS. MYRICK. All seemed fine, so I continue teaching regrouping, and the next thing I know, he started shouting, "Shut up boy, that's why you eat your momma booty."

DJ DRIZZLE. See.

MS. MYRICK. Right! Now, I'm pissed. I was being gentle with my words and all the textbook strategies. I called the house and told mom that he needed to stay home for the remainder of the day.

DJ DRIZZLE. Wait, you bypassed the principal?

MS. MYRICK. You have to do what you have to do in those situations. He'd clearly went to the office without consequences, so I had to handle it, or I was going to be institutionalized.

DJ DRIZZLE. Sounds like y'all need some more help in the elementary school.

MS. MYRICK. You're right! Middle school doesn't seem too bad, after all.

DJ DRIZZLE. I never thought you would utter those words. Well, you delivered as promised and just in time because we are out of time. As always, it's a pleasure to have you. So sad we only have one more session, but I look forward to an awesome ending. Until then, that's all in the Dirty, Dirty.

[*Fades out.*]

Session 15

DJ DRIZZLE. It's hot outside! I know you are cooling off in this blazing weather. It's Sunday afternoon, and you know what that means, we are spreading the jams and hanging out with our favorite teacher. It's almost time for summer break, and we are sad this is our last session with Ms. Myrick. I know y'all have been enjoying the tales of Ms. Myrick and her students, and so have I. It's probably one of my favorite sessions within the radio segments.

MS. MYRICK. Back then, they didn't want me.

DJ DRIZZLE. Ah, here you go. You going to miss those kids?

Ms. Y'all, I know I'm supposed to be extremely excited about this week being the last week and all. I certainly am, but Lord, I'm dreading it all in the same sentence. Those jokers will be all in my space. Last week, they kept crying, hugging me, sneaking hugs, staring at me being all awkward trying to get me to make eye contact so they could attack. They wouldn't play at recess. They kept trying to sit at my feet. They kept saying, "Ms. Myrick," all day. I can't handle this pressure from little kids. I just want them to be normal and say, "See ya later!" Then they had the audacity to say, "Ms. Myrick you only have one more day to give us some attention."

DJ DRIZZLE. You know you like them hugs!

MS. MYRICK. Maybe, but I ain't about to be soft on this radio station!

DJ DRIZZLE. Are those feelings coming out?

MS. MYRICK. Okay, you are doing too much. Let me tell this story before you get carried away.

DJ DRIZZLE. Okay, go ahead.

MS. MYRICK. It was Awards Day last week, and you know I'm trying to be great. Just want to ease out of here without a glitch.

DJ DRIZZLE. I just don't see that happening with this group.

MS. MYRICK. You knew! I have this crazy parent that comes around every now and then, straight looney toon. I've hidden in another class so he wouldn't talk to me for an hour straight.

DJ DRIZZLE. That's ridiculous.

MS. MYRICK. I just didn't want to be bothered. He had alcohol on his breath, and if the male teacher ain't across the hall, I'm not trying to be in a room with him.

DJ DRIZZLE. It's like that?

MS. MYRICK. Yea, but anyway. At Awards Day, the parent was there being extra, but I was able to speak to the grandmother.

DJ DRIZZLE. So, wait. This student's father and the father's mother was there?

MS. MYRICK. Yes, keep up. So, the grandmother looked me deep in my eyes and said, "Thank you for taking care of my grandbaby and his reading."

DJ DRIZZLE. Well, that was a pleasant ending.

MS. MYRICK. Yea, until she doubled back and said, "And, sorry for my rude ass child," the one she gave birth. She kissed my cheek and gave me a hug. That meant the world to me. She acknowledged her crazy child but was thankful for her grandbaby.

DJ DRIZZLE. That was even better.

MS. MYRICK. And plus, it always feels good to get a good ole grandma hug!

DJ DRIZZLE. I think it's dope that you have the courage to tell these stories.

MS. MYRICK. Yea, it's hard to tell stories about other children, but sometimes it's just a relief to be able to unwind and release. We, teachers, don't get that often. The government treats teachers like the scum on the bottom of a shoe. Certain laws prevent you from telling certain stories, but I figured it could be done tastefully.

DJ DRIZZLE. Well, you know I want to bring you back for another season.

MS. MYRICK. Of course, I will be back, but I requested to move to a different grade level, so the content may be a little different.

DJ DRIZZLE. You're just trying to sneak back to middle school.

Ms. Myrick. Maybe, but for now, elementary will do.

DJ Drizzle. You heard it here first. Ms. Myrick will be back with more of her teacher stories, and we can't wait to see you again in August. Aye, Mih My, drop that beat one last time.

Ms. Myrick. You're listening to DJ Drizzle and Ms. Myrick at WX-309. If you see me in the streets, say what's up! Drizzle let's Hit the Quan really quick.

DJ Drizzle. Oh, don't tempt me with a good time. You heard what she said, "Hit the Quan."

Made in the USA
Columbia, SC
07 September 2020